A NOVELLA BY VALERIE DEVONE-GRIMES

Misty

A TALE OF PAIN TRANSFORMED INTO TRIUMPH

Copyright © 2024 Valerie Devone-Grimes

Title: Misty

Hardcover ISBN: 978-1-965757-20-8

Paperback ISBN: 978-1-965757-18-5

E-book: 978-1-965757-19-2

Printed in the United States of America.

Dedication

This book is dedicated to every woman that had to migrate to America to escape violence and turmoil in their native lands. In hoping for a better life, they instead were met with challenges along the way.

Bio

Valerie Devone-Grimes is a remarkable woman who has mastered a variety of skills. From crafting to jewelry-making and cooking to poetry, she is an expert in all these art forms. She seeks out things that bring her joy, and it shows as we have watched her bloom over the years, from decorating cakes to designing wedding accessories. She has given demo cooking classes as well as taught poetry classes in 2008. To celebrate her students' success, a huge party was thrown in their honor.

Furthermore, she works with children in daycare centers and adults at one of the Queens Public Libraries, teaching them the basics of reading and writing. Her goal is for those she helps with library programs to create educational projects.

After completing high school, Valerie attended college for two years before joining a nursing home in Flushing, Queens, where she worked for 26 years. Utilizing her creative abilities while working there, she sold dinners, held bake sales, and hosted yard sales. Mrs. Grimes is quite active in her community.

She married Rodney Grimes several years ago, and together they have one son, Isaiah Grimes. Family is always at the center of Valerie's life, providing her with motivation and inspiration to achieve her goals. She made appearances on QPTV, tackling various topics such as cooking, crafts, and poetry and giving helpful advice throughout each show.

It is no wonder she earned the nickname "Cake Lady"; everyone knows about her delicious homemade cakes! We are delighted to welcome you to this incredible adventure as we delve into the pages of her thought-provoking tale. Get ready for a reading experience that you will not soon forget.

Through her prolific writing abilities, she has created a diverse collection of over forty-five books in different genres. However, she is now taking on a new venture: crafting stories of excitement and adventure that can be enjoyed by readers from all around the world.

Contents

Introduction

Within minutes, her village was destroyed, leaving nothing but ashes and rubble. Misty was faced with the decision of whether to remain where she was, or risk being the next victim of the rebels. She chose to make a run for her life to escape the brutal massacres that had taken place in her village. In one devastating moment, she realized that she had lost everything that she held so dear. Unable to shake off the nightmares of the sight of her parents and best friend's lifeless bodies, Misty was haunted by the memories of them every waking moment. With no one left to turn to, she had no other choice but to start life over.

With nothing more than a battered suitcase filled with tattered rags and meager possessions. She refused to give up, determined to make something of herself. Her aunt, a beacon of hope in her shattered world, helped her make plans to escape to America from her war-torn home in Ghana, West Africa.

It was a daunting journey, but she never once wavered in her determination to leave the pain and tragedy behind. As she arrived at her new college, she met her roommate, Carol. The two girls could not have been more different, but they quickly formed a bond. As she adapted to her new life, Misty had to confront the painful memories of her past. Despite her hesitance, Misty found herself in therapy, trying to heal from the trauma that haunted her. But amidst the turmoil, a chance encounter with a young man named Johnathan in the college cafe changed everything.

The journey may have been difficult, but she has emerged stronger and more determined than ever before. And now, she stands on the brink of a new chapter in her life. One will be captivated by the incredible story of this remarkable young woman.

Misty

A TALE OF PAIN TRANSFORMED INTO TRIUMPH

A Novella by

VALERIE DEVONE-GRIMES

1

From Tragedy to Triumph: Misty's Journey

Hello! My name is Misty. I live in a small village in Ghana, West Africa. One Friday morning, while I was fast asleep, noises of angry shouting men and gunshots rang out and awakened me. Frightened and confused I eased down to the floor and crawled behind a barrel and hid myself. After a few minutes there was silence. I eased to the door and carefully opened it only to find that in my disbelief that blood was dripping from my mother's chest. As I looked over to my father, a bullet hole could be seen in his skull leaving blood running down his face. My family had been brutally slaughtered while I was asleep.

Overwhelmed with grief, I ran away from the destruction of my family and home. Just as I was leaving, I noticed my best friend lying on the ground in front of her hut, eyes wide open and lost to the rebels. Tears ran down my face as I ran and wondered why their lives had been taken instead of mine. I eventually made it to my aunt's village, and when she asked me what happened, I could barely speak through the sobs as I described the tragic scenes of my village that had occurred.

It had been just ten days before my 17th birthday that I had received a full scholarship to New York City University and was about to depart for America, when the tragedy struck. My aunt assured me that I was safe and that everything would be ok.

After an arduous 12-hour journey followed by an 8-hour flight, we finally arrived in New York City for the first time. Misty quickly exchanges her currency and makes her way to the baggage claim area. After retrieving her luggage, she goes in search of someone that was holding a sign that read, "Misty" to take her to the university.

When she arrives at her destination, Misty's luggage wheel breaks off as she attempts to pull it out of the trunk. Frustrated, she reluctantly drags the three wheel luggage into the dorm, only to find that her room is no bigger than a matchbox! To make matters worse, she must share this tiny space with another student named Carol, who turns out to be very nice.

There was barely enough space for two people, let alone our belongings. However, there was a small refrigerator, which was perfect for us. We shared one big window in the room that gave us light and air. The room had bright lights, and a sweet scent that emanated from a vase of flowers that rested on the windowsill. Misty puts away her clothes and shoes while Carol fills up the closet space that was left.

That evening, we picked up our class schedules and found a meal plan and cafeteria. We then sat down and made rules for our room. Misty's dorm room, though small, would become her sanctuary. She decorated her side with reminders of home—colorful kente cloths, a small wooden carving of an elephant that her father had given her, and a few cherished photos. These items brought her a little comfort, but they also reminded her of all that she had lost.

At night, she would lie in bed, clutching the carved elephant, and whisper prayers to her parents, hoping that they could hear her from wherever they were. The silence of the dorm room at night was both soothing and sorrowful, amplifying her thoughts and feelings as she eventually drifted to sleep.

After talking to Carol, Misty was eager to explore the university. She had never seen a place like that before; she normally lived in homes with red clay and dirt floors and scant electricity, depending on the sunlight for school lessons; with wide eyes, she touched the walls and examined the art pieces hanging in the hallways. Wow! Here each student gets their own textbooks; and they don't have to share. Misty thought to herself that she could definitely get used to this. She spoke out loud and said this place wasn't so bad after all!

Despite the pain, Misty knew that she had to keep going. Her parents had always emphasized the importance of education, and she was determined to honor their memory by excelling in her studies. She had been accepted into one of the most prestigious colleges in the United States. It was a dream that had once seemed out of reach, but now a reality. As Misty grappled with the challenges of adapting to a new country and a rigorous academic schedule, she had to push herself forward. The prospect of success seemed both exhilarating and terrifying at the same time to Misty.

As Misty started her classes, she felt out of place because the cultural differences were overwhelming with students from all different walks of life. In Ghana, community was everything, the people looked out for each other, always finding someone to talk to or share a meal with. As she observed, the bustling campus was filled with students that seemed to move at different paces, but with a purpose that she couldn't quite grasp. They spoke quickly, laughed easily, and seemed to fit in effortlessly, which Misty envied.

She struggled to keep up in her classes, not because she lacked intelligence but because of the weight of her grief that she carried with her made it hard for her to focus. The ache and longing for her parents gnawed at her, and a constant reminder of how far away she was from home and the little family that she had left.

One of the hardest parts was dealing with the well-meaning but often insensitive comments from her peers. They would complain about trivial matters—bad grades, relationship drama, such as not getting into a party. Misty would force a smile, nodding along while her mind screamed at the unfairness of it all.

How could they understand the gravity of her loss? She wanted to shout at them to make them see that their problems paled in comparison to hers. But she knew that it would only isolate her further. Instead, she bottled up her feelings, presenting a facade of normalcy while her heart ached inside.

As tears started to roll down her cheeks, Carol stepped in and hugged her. At that moment, a university counselor passed by and asked if everything was alright. Not knowing what to say, Misty simply mentioned that she was looking for help as she was having trouble adjusting to college life as an excuse.

Mr. Larry then provided his number so they could arrange an appointment, and he could offer the necessary support. Misty thought to herself, maybe he could come to her aid. The next day, Misty attended her classes—she had a full schedule of seven classes and did her homework at the library. Who should pop up but Mr. Larry? He was well-liked among the students. He reached in his pocket and pulled out a card and said to stop by anytime. Misty considered the invitation given by Mr. Larry to attend a group meeting with six other people at 2:45 pm on Saturday, and she agreed.

But in that moment of uncertainty, Misty thought to herself that she hoped she wasn't making a mistake, but deep down inside her heart, she knew that it was worth giving it a chance. As Misty walked into the university counseling center on Saturday, for the first time, her steps were hesitant. The large, imposing building had an air of intimidation. But she had heard from some of the other students that the therapy sessions were beneficial for her to learn to cope with her ordeal.

2

<u>Learning to Let Go in Order to Rebuild</u>

Dr. Laura was a specialist in helping people cope with tragedy and trauma through hypnosis and revisiting the occurrence of the trauma. She taught how to find closure from the trauma in order to live a productive life. Misty, after talking to Dr. Laura, and feeling comfortable, saw this as her chance to start over and gain some control over her life.

On her way back to the dorm for the day, Misty sees Carol. Her friend invites her to a house party for freshmen, but Misty declines. She would rather spend the evening pondering over all that Dr. Laura had said to her and then watch television until she falls asleep.

Carol explained that she heard the screaming from the other side of the room since they lived in the same dorm room. The morning couldn't come quick enough for both of them, because Misty had another meeting with Dr. Laura and the group that day.

Misty was uncertain whether to wear something from her village or bring an item that belonged to her parents. Sarcastically, Misty thought for a moment in weakness, "How could Quack help me? Maybe I shouldn't go." Thought Misty. But it was as if Carol heard her thoughts and hollered for her to go, adding that everything would be okay. Carol also replied that Misty wasn't the only one who had ever lost someone close to her heart.

She didn't know this, but Carol had lost her uncle Joe years ago right in front of her. He was taking her to school one morning, when a car came speeding down the street and lost control hitting her uncle as he had picked her up in a split second to put her on the sidewalk before being runned over.

By the time the ambulance came to take him to the hospital, he had died leaving a frantic and terrified little girl to witness it. How could I ever forget that? My uncle and I shared many great memories together, he was like a father to me. Carol shared with Misty her traumatic experience that day and said, "See, I can relate to you! Even now I sometimes see his face in my dreams, bringing a smile to my face but sadness to my heart." "Wow! You never mentioned that to me before. It's true; you never know what someone else has experienced in their lives." Said Misty.

The clock read 1:30 p.m. "I need to get going," said Misty, leaving Carol alone in their room. Because her meeting was several buildings over and on the fifth floor. "We had a sign-in sheet and did a roll call of the people that had attended the meeting. There were ten people that were sitting in a circle that looked like they were lost in their thoughts meditating.

Suddenly, Dr. Laura enters the room and commands the attention of everyone present. "We all went around introducing ourselves, and when my name was called, everyone welcomed me. Dr. Laura then addressed the class, explaining that today's assignment was to write about how the nightmares make us feel. We also had a partial class session where we did hypnotherapy together. It lasted for three hours, and within that time we learned how to breathe properly, speak about our traumas. We also learned how to let go of the bad energy in our lives and to bring in the good energy." Recollected Misty.

The day after, while Misty was alone in her dorm room, she wrote in her journal about all the new things she had experienced that week. Misty was certain that she would be returning back for another session with Dr. Laura.

Dr. Laura requested for her to come back for a follow-up session to discuss how she could heal herself from the nightmares that she had been suffering with. What an emotional ride it has been! Dr. Laura advised her to do some deep breathing exercises and yell out what was bothering her. She was told that crying would help release her from the psychological confinement that was holding her. "You didn't do anything wrong, dear; this is beyond your control." Said Dr. Laura soothingly. "Let go of them and free yourself from the mental prison you've built up in your mind. You don't hear the sounds of the rebels or gunshots as your parents are being slaughtered, as you're walking it out. But, it will help you come to terms with it. Now is the time for you to look at it with a different perspective and look at it as you have something to be grateful for, and that your life was spared by the grace of God. Look how far you've come for the opportunity to be here to get your education, just as your parents had arranged." Said Dr. Laura.

As the semester progressed Misty accomplished great things and now it was time to go on summer break. She managed to earn a 3.75 GPA for her first year. Misty talked of aiming for 4.0 next year.

During the summer Misty decided that she would stay on campus as she had nowhere else to go. Carol offered Misty to come home with her so that she wouldn't be on campus alone. Misty responded gratefully. " You will love my mom; she makes chocolate brownies that'll make you swoon! She's been making them since I was a kid." Said Carol.

Misty visited Dr. Laura's office one last time and shared that she would be leaving campus for the summer but would return and continue working on her emotional issues after the summer. She also shared with Dr. Laura that her walls were beginning to give way. Dr. Laura replied, "Alright then, enjoy your summer. I'll see you when the new semester begins. Dr. Laura was pleased to hear that report from Misty and encouraged her to maybe find a male friend to talk to on campus. However, she cautioned Misty to ensure that the relationship stayed platonic, especially, if she wasn't ready for any physical intimacy.

Misty agreed with Dr. Laura and a few days later, she summoned up the courage to talk to Jonathan, the librarian. "Wow! I've met someone new for the first time. He is kind and cute. But, as quickly as she said that Misty says to herself, we aren't here for boys."

This was her first time speaking openly to a young man, because she felt in her heart that she needed someone else besides Carol to talk and laugh with. When Carol learned about Jonathan, she was eager to meet him and discovered that he was from the United States, but not from her hometown. Johnathan is someone that she enjoys talking to, and they sometimes go to the movies together, but nothing more than that.

Misty stopped by Jonathan's dorm room before leaving to tell him that she was going home with Carol for spring break. Jonathan hadn't expected her to do that, but thought she would stay on campus. But Misty had other plans for the break. She told him that she'd been pushing herself hard with schoolwork and needed a break.

Teasing a little, she asked if he minded her going away, assuring him it would only be for six weeks before seeing his handsome face again.

Misty returned to her dorm room to start packing for her upcoming trip. Carol then reassured her, saying she could stay in the spare bedroom at home with a large flat-screen television. She also mentioned that there was a swimming pool in the backyard. Misty relaxed a little thinking that she was about to have fun over the summer.

However, what Carol didn't mention was that she liked drinking when no one else was home. She also had a physical relationship with someone back home but wasn't telling her about it.

On Thursday morning, they arrived at Carol's house and were greeted with a warm embrace. Afterwards, Misty followed Carol's directions to the bedroom where she'd be staying and unpacked her stuff, and then she went down to the kitchen to have dinner with Carol's family.

After dinner, Carol had promised to take Misty and her friends to the mall, but what Misty didn't know was that she wasn't planning on paying for anything. While at the store, and to Misty's amazement; she saw Carol do something very unlike the person that she met and knew back at college. Suddenly, it dawned on her what Carol was doing at the stores—slipping items into her clothing. Misty quickly went and asked Carol what she was doing, and said, "Your mom provided us with a black card just in case we wanted to buy something."

Quickly, remembering that in her country, theft was severely punished—by having one's hands cut off. She told Carol to take her home, not approving of that kind of behavior which she had seen. They drove back in silence, Misty gazing out the window at the pedestrians on the street. Now they were home, and neither of them spoke to one another. When Mom returned home from work, she was puzzled by the hushed atmosphere. Carol begged her not to bring it up. It was almost humorous to see how well Carol was able to get away with her antics.

It was dinner time, and they all sat down together as a family. Misty had a flashback of her family sitting in the hut together at mealtime. She treasured those memories in her heart and She snapped back into the conversation with Carol's Mom.

After dinner, Misty turned in early, as she drifted off to sleep, she dreamt of her hometown village, with her best friend waving to her from afar. She woke up the next morning, confused by the vision she had seen.

The next day, Carol and Misty made breakfast together and made funny-looking pancakes. The weekend came quickly, and they planned a pool party in the backyard. A few friends came over; some smoked while others popped pills. Misty couldn't understand why someone would do something so stupid just for entertainment's sake.

Misty didn't understand why Carol was so into these seemingly trivial activities. She had no idea that Carol was concealing her identity while she was in college and was doing all the ridiculous things she did for fun. Carol seemed to be the perfect role model when she was at college. "How wrong could I have been?" Thought Misty.

Misty carried on with her day as planned, spending time by the pool. She helped herself to a plate of grilled food and kept sipping on seltzer water. She was having a peaceful time, splashing her feet in the water, when the guy, Peter, approached her to introduce himself. He said he felt like they could relate to each other. However, another girl spoke up, warning Misty not to waste her time on him, as Peter was known for his flirtatiousness with girls.

It's almost like Misty couldn't escape the guys who constantly hit on her. The way of life that Carol chooses to lead is drastically different from what Misty does. She enjoyed taking care of Carol, even though it wasn't her first choice of activity. The idea of having sex with someone she had never met or knew seemed out of the question for Misty; she held herself to high standards like that.

Still seated by the pool, Misty soon heard her phone ring; it was Jonathan calling her for the first time in almost three weeks. Hearing his voice once again warmed her heart. They spoke for a few hours until Carol appeared, looking for Misty. Carol reminded her that she was at a pool party. "Don't be a party-pooper about it!" Carol exclaimed. Jonathan then asked Misty what she was talking about, to which Misty replied that she was at a pool party.

Jonathan said before hanging up, "I miss you, Misty". Misty also conveyed her own affection for him. His voice echoed through the phone as they spoke, their longing evident in every word. Misty couldn't help but feel a pang of sadness. "I really miss you!" Said Misty. She had longed to stay on campus for spring break and spend more time with him. She couldn't help but express her own affection for him too; the distance only intensified their feelings for each other.

They were both relieved that their reunion would happen very soon. She places her earphones back in her ears and continues to listen to music with her eyes closed, as she lay on a blow-out float in the water. At that moment, nothing mattered but the peaceful serenity and the thought of soon being reunited with Jonathan.

3

New Semester, New Challenges

The young ladies had little more than a week before the new semester resumed, and they were busy preparing. They laundered their clothes, grabbed school supplies, and stocked up on canned goods, teas, and snacks. Although the cafeteria would replenish their food supply when they returned to the campus, but they wanted something in their refrigerator for late-night snacking.

Carol said to Misty, "When mom is free, she could take us back to the campus." Misty replied, "That sounds great, but in the meantime, we can check our schedules for the upcoming semester." Misty shared the news with Carol that she needed to achieve a 4.0 GPA this semester to keep her scholarship. "We all knew that money doesn't grow on trees, so it was time to buckle down and get serious if I wanted to succeed." Thought Misty. Misty and Carol had made a bet, that whoever failed to make a 4.0 GPA this semester would have to clean their room from then until the end of December. They sealed the deal with a handshake, and the challenge was set.

The day arrived when Carol's mom drove them back to their dorm. She parked the car and assisted her daughter as they made their way back inside. Unfortunately, the electricity had been out for three days already, leaving their room lit only by sunlight and LED lights, and at night emergency lighting.

The next morning, the college's repairmen arrived to restore the power to the building, eliciting cheers from the girls and other students. On that Thursday, classes began, and they couldn't have been more relieved that the lights were on again on the campus. Plus, "We need the lights to get started on our academic quest if we were going to make the challenge." Said Carol.

"I'm gonna go and meet up with Jonathan at the library; we agreed to meet for coffee. We will catch up later."

Said Misty. Carol replied, "Okay! I'm just gonna run to the school's store really quick and pick up a math textbook." "Sounds like a plan," Misty replied. "Let's hook up around seven-ish for dinner."

Misty beamed when she saw Johnathan, giving him a big kiss as they embraced. She savored the scent of his cologne and remembered how much she'd missed it these past few months.

They settled onto the couch, and Misty inquired about what he had been up to during their time apart. Johnathan replied that he'd worked in the library to help pay for tuition and gone to the movies a couple of times, but nothing else too exciting. He also spent time helping his parents around their home and returning back to campus.

Misty shared her story next, explaining how things had not gone as planned on her picnic with Carol and her friends. She hadn't expected them to be into stealing, doing drugs, and partying late into the night.

Misty continued by saying that Carol's parents had been very loving towards her as she was growing up. However, they were still very strict. But she had seen things that she wouldn't have seen in her own home back in Ghana, and never imagined from Carol's, either. Carol seemed to get away with whatever she wanted at home. Johnathan was astounded; he had never known that side of her.

She kept her true character concealed. I asked Jonathan not to share this with Carol; after all, we have to live in the same dorm room. "Enough about that, though; give me a kiss over here." Said Misty. As they talked, reclining on the loveseat snuggled together, It was nearly 6:45 p.m. when Misty remembered that she promised to meet up with Carol around seven o'clock for dinner that night.

After saying their farewells for the evening, they made plans to get together again soon. As she started walking away, Misty blew a kiss in Johnathan's direction and said, "See ya later; call me." Misty met up with Carol, and curiosity piqued about what they'd be doing. Suddenly, Mom showed up and provided meatballs and spaghetti, as well as garlic bread.

Grateful for Mom's thoughtfulness, the two settled down to enjoy their meal together before watching a movie and eventually dropping off into a slumber. The following day, classes started very early - 8:00 a.m. Carol remarked that she had a class at 8:45 a.m. and couldn't risk being late. Misty reminded her of their agreement; Misty's classes didn't start until 9:30 a.m. "Lucky you," Carol replied.

"Don't make it so easy for me to win this challenge!" she teased. Carol shrugged and replied, "It's just the first day back; my mom said practice makes perfect!" She laughed as they headed off in different directions. "Ha ha," laughed Carol.

The time to return to the class finally was here. Once in the classroom the familiar sound of chairs scraping against the linoleum floor and the rustling of notebooks being opened filled the air as they settled into their seats for their first lesson. "See you later today after class." Said Misty to her friend sitting next to her with her textbook already open in front of her. "Looking around the room, I couldn't help but feel a sense of determination and nervousness bubbling within me.

I knew that this semester would bring new challenges and demands, especially when it came to taking notes and studying for the exams. But with each challenge came an opportunity to learn and grow." Misty whispered to herself.

Despite facing a tragic past, Misty's unwavering drive and resilience radiated through her whenever she sat in the classroom and participated. As classes went on her grades were a testament to her perseverance, even in the face of adversity.

As she delved deeper into her studies, Misty discovered hidden talents and a passion for advocating for her home and its people. Each new discovery ignited a fire within her heart, fueling a purpose within and giving her hope that she could make a difference in the world. And as she looked towards the future, Misty knew that maintaining a 4.0 GPA every semester would be a true catalyst of reaching and fulfilling that purpose.

Driven by an unrelenting passion to make a positive impact in the African communities, Misty throws herself into the work of "Lift One & Help One." It was an organization that supported and empowered those in need. It resonated deep within her soul.

As an American, Carol has never experienced such struggles firsthand; the thought alone sends shivers down Misty's spine. In the land of the free, breaking the law is met with harsh punishment and imprisonment. This ideal of freedom should be safeguarded at all costs, yet it is being violated without consequence. These thoughts swirl around in Misty's mind as she reflects on the deeply troubling state of affairs in her homeland.

Yet, despite all of society's progress, how is it possible that slavery still exists in her country? Questioned Misty. In today's world, families like the Ghanaians are often torn apart or even killed over simple matters of religious practices. The gravity of these injustices hit Misty hard, causing her voice to rise in despair.

But in her quest to change the world and bring attention to the problems that her people suffered, Misty encounters severe setbacks and fierce opposition. She is committed to using her voice and knowledge in the future to build a better tomorrow. As the sun sets on that evening, Misty eagerly makes her way to the cultural community meetings. Amongst a sea of African brothers and sisters from her country and others, she finds comfort and strength in their shared experiences.

The weekend finally arrived, and a sense of excitement and anticipation filled the air. "How would I spend my time with Carol, someone I haven't seen much of lately due to our busy schedules? We always seem to be passing each other by in a blur, rushing off to class, or appointments. But this weekend, I was determined to make it count.

Finally, we just decided to relax and enjoy each other's company without any distractions. The thought made us both giggle like schoolgirls. This would be a weekend to remember, for sure." Thought Misty.

"What should we start with?" Carol asked, her eyes wide with anticipation. "How about some classic black-and-white films?" Misty suggested, glancing at the clock, which read 5:30 p.m. "I'll make the drinks, and you make the popcorn," she continued, a mischievous grin spreading across her face. "Just don't burn the popcorn like last time, Carol." Said Misty "I won't, I promise," Carol replied with a chuckle.

"Let's grab a big bowl from the cafeteria for the popcorn," Misty said, already gathering her things to head out. "Now that is a great idea," Carol exclaimed as they hurriedly got dressed and went to the cafeteria. It was shaping up to be an unforgettable movie night with their best friend by their side.

Every night before going to bed, unbeknownst to Carol, Misty diligently kept a journal book that she daily poured her heart into its pages. She journals her good days, bad days, and in between days. Misty also chronicled the emotional account of losing her loved ones, while navigating a new life in a foreign country at college, and even the most exhilarating moments of her young life.

This was her coping mechanism, a way to navigate the ups and downs of her current life. But, she had made the conscious decision to take control and shape the rest of her journey to one that she could be very proud of. Though every day was and remains a challenge for Misty, she knew that she had to take the step of pushing what happened to her parents and the others aside. She had to focus and maintain her mental health for her academic performance.

Misty has been studying hard day and night in order for her to make it through the year. Her professors were impressed by her quick grasp of the material and her ability to handle herself with such poise.

Misty reassured herself that she had this in the bag, confident in her dedication to her studies and the sacrifices that she had made, including time spent with friends and Jonathan, all for the sake of her academic success. She could feel the anticipation building as she eagerly awaited her final grade for the semester. Had she met her goal of a perfect 4? Thought Misty.

Recalling, her first semester was a blur of textbooks, lectures, and endless assignments with each day feeling like a battle. She spent hours in the library, pushing herself to read through the materials and her tears at times forcing herself to understand. Her professors were kind but firm, and while they offered her help, they couldn't truly understand the depths of her pain and struggle.

The language barrier, though not insurmountable, added another layer of difficulty. Academic jargon was challenging enough without having to translate it in her head before comprehending it. Every page she turned and every note that she took felt like a small victory against the tide of emotional despair. Her pain and struggles became the solid foundation and drive for her growth. Therapy sessions with Dr. Laura was a crucial tool in her healing process, where their sessions became a lifeline for Misty. She could unload her burdens without fear of judgement.

During this time, her friendship with Carol, Jonathan, and Dr. Laura grew deeper. Carol was patient, empathetic, and genuinely interested in helping Misty navigate her new life. She also introduced her to mindfulness and meditation techniques, helping her to find other ways to manage her anxiety and intrusive thoughts. They would often take walks around the campus, talking about everything from Misty's classes to Jonathan to Ghana. When speaking of

Johnathan, Misty saw that was a pillar of strength that she could lean and depend on to lift her up.

Over the weeks and months Misty's platform of cultural involvement grew wider, and her resources expanded, allowing her to reach even more people with her message. It was then that Misty truly understood the power of storytelling, and she made the decision to write a memoir sharing her incredible journey.

She hoped to inspire countless others to never give up on their dreams and to always believe in themselves. Despite not expecting a large turnout, she was amazed by the dedicated few who came to listen and support one another.

The committed individuals help spread the word by creating eye-catching flyers to distribute throughout the campus. Even those living around the campus stop by to listen to the powerful discussions that took place at every meeting.

4

<u>Through the Ashes: A Journey of Strength</u>

Although Misty had always been resilient, the previous year had put her to the test in ways she never would have predicted. Her dreams were now haunted by memories of her village. She would never forget the blackened remnants and the stench of the smoke. She felt emptiness in her heart from losing her parents and friend in the massacre. She would frequently catch herself gazing at old pictures, trying to recall every little detail of their appearances, their voices, and the feel of their embraces. Though she lived with the nagging presence and anguish all the time, she allowed herself to be grateful for her life.

But the relief was temporary. The holidays were especially tough. While her classmates went home to their families, Misty stayed on campus. The dorms, usually buzzing with activity, were eerily quiet. She spent Christmas alone, eating instant noodles and watching the snow fall outside of the window. The solitude was crushing, and she felt the pangs of homesickness more acutely than ever. She missed the warmth of Ghana, the festive celebrations, and, most of all, her parents' comforting presence. The contrast between her vibrant memories of home and the cold, silent campus was stark.

Determined not to let the loneliness consume her, Misty decided that it was time for some extracurricular activities to occupy some of her time and mind. So, she joined a dance class and was immediately enthralled with what she saw. The instructor's name was Ms. Rodriguez, who looked just as young as her students. Ms. Rodriquez quickly drew Misty into the class and wasted no time in doing so. There were several students practicing their movements and luring her in. She wanted to be as free as they appeared in dance. Her dance instructor, Ms. Rodriguez noticed Misty's talent and dedication. She took her under her wing, offering extra practice sessions and encouraging her to even perform in the upcoming showcase. "Dance is a language of its own, so use it to tell your story." Said Ms.

Rodriquez. And so, Misty did. She poured her heart into her dance, letting the movements speak of her pain, her loss, and her resilience.

The showcase was a turning point for her. As she performed, she felt a sense of release, whether she was practicing or in a showcase, which was a momentary freedom from the chains of her past. Misty later took on leadership roles in the dance club, mentoring younger students and choreographing performances. She also joined another cultural organization on campus, connecting with other international students who understood the complexities of adapting to a new environment.

These activities provided her with a sense of purpose and community, something she had desperately missed. Being a vocal activist on campus had solidified her place in this new environment, things had begun to look promising for Misty.

Her dance instructor, Ms. Rodriguez, noticed Misty's talent and dedication. She took Misty under her wing, offering extra practice sessions and encouraging her to even perform in the upcoming showcase "Dance is a language of its own," Ms. Rodriguez would say. "Use it to tell your story." And so, Misty did. She poured her heart into her dance, letting the movements speak of her pain, her loss, and her resilience. The showcase was a turning point for her. As she performed, she felt a sense of release, whether she was practicing or in a showcase a momentary freedom from the chains of her past.

Feeling a little balance in her life, Misty threw herself into her studies with even more fervor. She set up a strict schedule, balancing her classes, homework, and dance practice. She attended every therapy session she could, seeking help from her professors and trying to bridge the gaps in her understanding. Slowly, her grades began to improve. She found that the more she immersed herself in her work, the less time she had to dwell on her sorrow. The structure and routine provided a much-needed distraction from her grief.

Carol later introduced Misty to mindfulness and meditation techniques, helping her find ways to also manage her lingering anxiety and intrusive thoughts. They would often go for walks around the campus, talking about everything from Misty's classes to her memories of Ghana. Carol shared her own struggles, creating a bond of mutual understanding. Carol's presence had become a comforting constant in her tumultuous world, providing both guidance and companionship.

Misty started to open up more to her classmates and shared her story, finding that talking about her experiences helped to lessen the burden. They were supportive, offering her kindness and understanding. She realized that she wasn't as alone as she had thought and that there were people who cared about her and wanted to see her succeed. The connections she formed became a vital part of her support system.

The turning point came during a particularly grueling exam period. Misty had three major exams in one week, and the pressure was overwhelming. She found herself slipping back into old patterns, struggling to concentrate, and feeling the weight of her grief more intensely. One night, as she sat in the library, tears streaming down her face, she received a text from Carol: "You are stronger than you think. Remember why you started this journey."

Misty thought about her parents and the sacrifices they had made to give her a better life. She remembered her father's words, "Education is the key to unlocking the golden door of freedom." With renewed determination, she tackled her studies with everything she had.

The promise she had made to her parents served as a beacon, guiding her through the darkest moments. Misty quickly pushed the memories that were threatening to overwhelm her again to the side, because it was exam week, and she needed to be focused. Her father's words had to take precedent over the trauma.

When the exam results came in, Misty was stunned. She had not only passed all her exams but had also achieved some of the highest scores in her classes. Her hard work had paid off, and for the first time, she allowed herself to feel proud. She called Carol and Jonathan, who cheered and celebrated with her. They both reminded her of her ability and strength, "See, you're stronger than you think, Misty." Carol said. "Absolutely!" Said Jonathan.

This victory was a turning point for Misty. It showed her that she could overcome any obstacle if she put her mind to it. She began to approach her challenges with a new mindset, viewing them not as insurmountable barriers but as opportunities to grow and prove her resilience, as her parents would want her to. She began to believe in herself even more, a feeling that had been a little in the distance.

Misty felt proud of herself going into her junior year. She came a long way from being the terrified young new lady who arrived in the US, who was overwhelmed by doubt and grief. Misty was well on her way to creating a brand-new, and meaningful life for herself that was full of caring relationships and positivity. But her journey was far from being over.

5

<u>From Fear to Fortitude</u>

*M*isty's junior year began with a whirlwind of events and emotions. She had just settled into her new dorm, embraced the rigorous demands of her classes, and found solace in the companionship of her friends. The days were a blur of studying, late-night conversations, and the occasional social gathering that offered a brief respite from her academic pressures. Among her circle of friends was Johnathan, who had become a very significant part of her life. Their connection had grown stronger over time, blossoming into a deep and meaningful relationship.

One crisp autumn evening, after a long day of lectures and hours spent in the library, Misty and Jonathan found themselves alone in his apartment. The atmosphere was warm and inviting, with dim lighting casting a soft glow around the room. As the evening progressed, their conversation was filled with laughter and intimate revelations and had evolved into a moment of passion. For a brief time, they lost themselves in each other, forgetting about the outside world and the pressures of their lives.

However, the morning brought a harsh reality that dawned on Misty, when she awakened with a sense of unease. The fleeting moment of passion now loomed over her like a dark cloud. She couldn't shake the nagging fear that she might be pregnant. The thought terrified her.

She had worked tirelessly to get to where she was, and a pregnancy could potentially derail all her plans and dreams. The anxiety was overwhelming, and her thoughts spiraled out of control. What would she do if she were pregnant? How would she take care of the baby? How would she manage her studies, her scholarship, and the future she had envisioned for herself?

Misty's mind raced as she tried to process the possibility. The fear gnawed at her, making it difficult to concentrate on anything else. Pacing the floor while uttering words of disbelief awakened Jonathan to a frantic Misty. "What's going on Misty? Why are you upset and pacing? Jonathan asked. Her words were but a mixed-up soup bowl of phrases to the point where she needed to leave. Misty quickly grabbed her belongings and ran out of the apartment leaving Jonathan alone, shocked and confused.

She needed to get away and talk to someone to find some form of clarity. She reached out to her trusted Dr. Laura, her therapist and confidante, who had been a steady source of support since their first meeting. Dr. Laura had a unique way of making Misty feel heard and understood, no matter what the circumstances were. Misty hoped that sharing her fears with her would help alleviate some of the anxiety that was now consuming her.

When Misty arrived at Dr. Laura's office, she could barely hold back her tears. She recounted the events of the previous night, her voice trembling with fear and uncertainty. Dr. Laura listened attentively, her expression compassionate and understanding. She provided Misty with a comforting presence, reassuring her that they would face any challenge together.

After a long and heartfelt conversation, Dr. Laura suggested that Misty take a pregnancy test to confirm her suspicions. The waiting period was excruciating. Each passing minute felt like an eternity as Misty anxiously awaited the results. When the day finally came for Misty to take the test, she was a bundle of nerves. Misty also confided in Jonathan about her concerns after realizing that this wasn't all about her. Jonathan reassured her that everything was going to be alright.

He wanted her to know that he was there with her, and they would go through this together. Her hands trembled as she held the test kit with her heart pounding in her chest. Jonathan too, was nervous, but refused to show it in front of Misty, because she had enough to deal with already.

Tucked inside the bathroom, she followed the pregnancy test kit instructions carefully, her mind filled with a mixture of hope and dread. The minutes that followed seemed to be some of the longest of their lives. She watched the test strip intently, waiting for the results to appear. Upon receiving the outcome, Misty felt immense relief—she wasn't pregnant. She exhaled a sigh of relief, then went to share the news with Jonathan. The weight that had been pressing down on their shoulders lifted, and they could finally breathe again.

The experience had left a deep mark on her and Jonathan, but especially her. She realized how close she had come to a situation that could have changed her, and Jonathan's lives forever. She made a vow to herself that she would never let fear control her actions, driving her to make irresponsible decisions.

In the days that followed, Misty shared more of her fears and experiences with her therapist. They talked about the pressures and challenges of college life, the complexities of relationships, and the importance of self-awareness and self-care. Misty focused on her studies with an even greater sense of determination to secure her future. It was always easy for Misty to share her experiences with Dr. Laura after learning of her own experiences with her own encounters with young men, providing a wealth of wisdom and perspective.

Dr. Laura's guidance once more helped Misty gain a deeper understanding of herself and her emotions. Some days their conversations would be filled with laughter, empathy, and on other days they were shared with tears. Through it all, Misty remained grateful for the support. As the semester progressed, Misty continued to excel academically.

Her hard work paid off, and she was able to maintain her 4.0 GPA, securing her scholarship and ensuring her path to graduation. The experience with Jonathan had also strengthened their bond, as they navigated the ups and downs of college life together. Misty's junior year was a period of significant growth and self-discovery. She had faced her fears head-on, learning valuable lessons about responsibility, trust, and resilience.

As she looked ahead to her senior year, Misty felt a sense of excitement and anticipation. She knew more challenges lay ahead, but she was prepared to confront them with courage and confidence. This chapter in her life, though filled with fear and uncertainty, ultimately strengthens her resolve and prepares her for the future. As

Misty continues her journey, she remains focused on her goals and dreams.

As summer approaches, Misty decided to take an internship to gain practical experience in her field of study. She secured a position at a prestigious firm, which meant she had to stay on campus over the summer. Jonathan also stayed back, taking summer classes to get ahead. The two of them enjoyed the quieter pace of the campus, which gave them more time to be together without the pressures of a full academic schedule. They explored the city, had picnics in the park, whenever they could.

The internship proved to be a challenging yet rewarding experience for Misty. She worked long hours, but the exposure to real-world applications of her studies was valuable. This opportunity allowed Misty to apply what she had learned in the classroom to practical problems, giving her a sense of accomplishment and a clearer vision of her career path.

Meanwhile, Jonathan's summer classes were intense but manageable. There were times that he wanted to visit

Misty at her office during her lunch break but couldn't, due to his demanding workload. As the summer came to an end, Misty reflected on the personal and professional growth she had experienced. The internship had provided her with a wealth of knowledge and confidence.

When the fall semester began, Misty and Jonathan settled back into their academic routines. The campus buzzed with the energy of students eager to start the new year. Misty's senior year brought with it a heavier course load and more demanding projects, but she was undeterred.

Throughout the year, Misty and Jonathan faced the typical ups and downs where there were moments of stress and tension, particularly as graduation was drawing closer. The pressures of completing job applications and future planning intensified. However, they always found their way back to each other, their commitment unwavering.

As winter approached, Misty began to feel the weight of an impending graduation. The thought of leaving the familiar environment of college and stepping into the unknown was both exciting and daunting. She spent countless hours perfecting her resume, preparing for interviews, and researching potential employers. Jonathan was equally busy, exploring graduate school options and applying for internships. They supported each other through the process, celebrating each other's successes.

One particularly challenging day, Misty received a rejection letter from a company that she had been excited about. The disappointment hit her hard, and she felt a wave of self-doubt wash over her. Johnathan, sensing her distress, took her out for a walk in the park. As they strolled through the crisp winter air, he reminded her of all her accomplishments and to look at the rejection letter and the company as not being the right fit for her. He also said that there would be other opportunities until she finds the company just for her.

As spring approached, the anticipation of graduation grew stronger. At the end of the semester, Misty and Jonathan attended a variety of parties and achievement ceremonies before graduation, celebrating their accomplishments with friends and family. The spirit of camaraderie and shared success was evident, leaving lasting impressions. However, Misty's parents were never far from her mind. This was a part of her life that she had always wanted them to see her achieve, but she knew they would be proud of her.

6

<u>Crossroads of the Heart</u>

Misty's final semester was a whirlwind of emotions and decisions. With just four credits remaining, the anticipation of graduation welled up in her like a volcano erupting on a Hawaiian island. On one side, there was the sweet promise of freedom and achievement; on the other side, there was a daunting void of uncertainty.

Misty knew that once she stepped off the campus grounds, she wouldn't have a home to return to. Her thoughts frequently drifted back to Ghana, to the village that was once home and had encompassed her entire world but now was reduced to ashes.

As graduation drew nearer, the question of what came next hung in the front of Misty's mind as a constant reminder. Dr. Laura had offered her a place to stay, a temporary refuge and promise of stability until she could find her own footing.

Jonathan also, on the other hand, represented the possibility of a new beginning. His dreams of a future together were enticing, promising a sense of belonging that Misty also craved deeply. He also was a constant reminder that life could be beautiful and filled with love.

There were moments when she felt a deep connection with him, a bond forged through shared experiences and mutual understanding. He had been there for her during some of her darkest moments, offering a shoulder to cry on and a hand to hold. Yet, there were also moments of doubt, when she wondered if she was good enough for him. Will she allow herself to be happy or will she run from what could be a wonderful life?

One evening, as they sat under the starry sky, he spoke of their relationship with such passion that it almost brought tears to her eyes. He envisioned a life where they would support each other through every challenge or situation, creating a vivid image of home filled with love and laughter.

Misty quickly shook herself out of second-guessing Jonathan and herself and chose to accept stability with Jonathan, instead of missing out on the best relationship that she could have had in her life.

His words were sincere, and his love for her was evident in every syllable. Then he reached for his pocket and to Misty's surprise, he presented her with a little red velvety box. Jonathan said to Misty, "This is for you, open it." Misty looked at Jonathan with tenderness as she opened the box slowly. It was the most beautiful unique ring that Misty had ever seen. It was designed with figures of a couple engraved on the sides with diamonds and onyx on the sides. He then got down on his knees and asked her if she would accept his hand in marriage and be his wife.

As she listened, her heart melted for the joy that he brought to her life. Her desire to have a home was coming to pass. Misty knew just what she wanted, and she answered him with a resounding yes. After having a warm embrace, they agreed to not jeopardize their future with any hasty decisions and would wait until after their graduation to have the wedding.

Misty's thoughts at times became a tangled web of fears and possibilities as the nights grow longer. She often found herself lying awake, staring at the ceiling, with her mind racing with what-ifs thoughts of marriage and graduation that were coming up soon.

The next morning Misty found herself at the campus flower garden where there were cascading water fountains and goldfish ponds. The tranquil, deserted garden was a sharp contrast to the hustle and bustle of the rest of the campus. As she casually walked along the paths, a sense of peace came over her.

The tranquility of the ponds mirrored her inner peace, revealing a woman on the brink of becoming someone that she never thought that she would become. When she was back home in Ghana thoughts of such a life were only a girl's imagination. She sat on the grass, bringing her knees to her breasts and allowing the tears she had been holding back to fall freely.

At that moment, Misty realized that no matter what lies ahead, she knew that her life was not the same as before. And that it would become a life that she created on her own. This realization brought another measure of peace, allowing her to see her life from a new perspective. It was not about choosing the safest or most exciting option, but about following her heart and trusting in her decision and newfound independence.

She spent the following days reflecting on everything she had experienced. This time with joy in her heart instead of experiencing the feelings of grief and sorrow. She knew that this would be what her parents would have wanted for her.

Graduation day arrived, and with a feeling of excitement Misty walked across the stage proudly to receive her diploma, and with a sense of accomplishment. As the applause of her peers, professors and Jonathan filled the atmosphere she couldn't help but to be happy. She had navigated the trials and tribulations, emerging stronger and more resolute.

After the ceremony, Misty gathered with her friends for final photos and farewells. Her therapy group, which had become a second family to her, showered her with love and well-wishes.

As Misty was preparing to leave the campus that had been her home for four years, she felt a little sad. The journey had been long and arduous, filled with heartache and triumph, but Misty survived. She now was ready to embrace the future, face its challenges and joys, and continue growing into the person she was meant to be. With a heart full of gratitude and hope, she left her dorm room for the last time determined not to look back on her painful past as she often did.

Settling down at Dr. Laura's home until her big day, Misty felt a sense of comfort and stability. The familiar warmth of Dr. Laura's presence and the cozy environment of her house created a sanctuary where Misty could focus on her future.

Dr. Laura continued to provide valuable support by encouraging Misty to always explore her dreams and passions. Their evenings were often filled with deep conversation, as Dr. Laura shared wisdom from her own life experiences, and Misty found it to be so encouraging to be in her mentor's presence.

Jonathan, meanwhile, remained a constant as his visits were frequent, filled with laughter and tenderness. They spent weekends exploring the city, discovering new places, and making memories of their own that added layers to their bond. Reflecting on her path, Misty realized that her story was one of transformation. Misty's new beginning was not defined by a single choice or relationship but by a series of actions that honored her true self.

7

A New Beginning

Misty started exploring graduate programs in counseling. She spent hours reading about different universities, their programs, and the opportunities they offered. The process was both exhilarating and overwhelming. Each program she considered brought her one step closer to her goal.

During this time Misty, Jonathan's mother and sister were also busy visiting bridal shops in search of her wedding dress as well as theirs. Misty enjoyed the attention and fuss that the bridal shop's attendants would give her, making her feel special. With a moment of being lost in her thoughts, Misty wished that her mother and best friend could've been there during this milestone in her life.

As she walked slowly through the bridal shop, Misty spotted a dress that spoke to her heart and said out loud, "This is it." She had found her wedding dress. After informing the attendant, she tried on the dress as she looked in the mirror and marveled at her reflection of how she looked in the dress.

Filled with happiness and excitement, Misty left the bridal shop with her soon to be family. She met up with Jonathan for dinner and exchanged their experiences of the day. They continued finalizing their wedding plans that were just three months away. Misty and Dr. Laura would make sure that they meet at least once a month to catch up on things, because of all the progress that she had made over the years.

Dr. Laura knew in her heart and approved of it, that it was time to release Misty from being her client and then move into the permanent role as friend. In the days to come Misty and Jonathan spent many days exploring venues, bakeries, and homes, so that they could have everything in place for the wedding.

As Misty continued her research and after applying to several graduate programs, one morning, she received an email from one of the universities. It was an acceptance letter from one of the prestigious universities that she had applied to their counseling programs. Her heart raced with excitement as she tore into the envelope and read the details. The program was everything that she had hoped for—comprehensive, challenging, and designed to equip her with the skills she needed to make a difference. She couldn't wait to share the news with Jonathan.

"Jonathan, I got in! I'm accepted!" Misty exclaimed as she rushed to him, waving the acceptance letter. His face lit up with joy. "Misty, that's incredible! I'm so proud of you," he said, pulling her into a tight embrace. They celebrated the good news together with his parents and sister. Misty knew that this was a significant step towards achieving her dreams, and she felt grateful for Jonathan's and his family's continued unwavering support.

The news came just two days before her wedding date. Suddenly, she began to feel a little overwhelmed with the wonderful things that were happening all at once.

Misty thought that she needed a minute to process everything that was happening. For a brief moment Misty couldn't believe things were happening so fast. "How could anyone be so fortunate?" She thought. Misty felt like she didn't deserve all the good fortune that she was having, when there was so much ugliness still back home in Ghana.

Misty suddenly shook off the negative thoughts and started preparing for her wedding day to the love of her life. On the day of the wedding Jonathan's mother and sister helped her get ready. Wanting to keep with tradition, she kept herself hidden from Jonathan until it was time to walk down the aisle to him. At the sight of Misty, the guest and Jonathan could be heard with excited words to describe her beauty. At the first sight of Misty, Jonathan was brought to tears at her striking radiant beauty.

The ceremony lasted less than an hour, and the newlyweds were off taking pictures as the guests were assembling in the catering hall for the reception. Jonathan and Misty danced the evening away with family and friends by their sides. Dr. Laura stood proudly watching, feeling almost as if Misty was her own daughter that she never had, as a lone tear glided down her cheek. For a wedding gift to Misty, Dr. Laura presented her with a cherished heirloom that she had once preserved for her daughter that never came. `

Misty's friends from the therapy group were thrilled for her. They had been her rock throughout their college years, and being there at her wedding and encouraging her meant the world. "We always knew you'd do great things, Misty," one of her friends said, raising a glass in her honor at the reception. Cheers and toasts went around the room from different supporters of Misty's and Jonathan's family and friends, which helped bring closure to their beautiful wedding day.

8

Home Sweet Home

Time went by in almost a blur for Misty and Jonathan, as they celebrated their fifth-year anniversary. Jonathan, being a successful investment broker, was starting his own firm. Misty on the other hand, was settled in her career as a counselor. Misty was a little unsettled after having experienced a few days of not feeling like herself.

One morning after getting dressed before going down for breakfast, the once welcomed smell of bacon and eggs that Jonathan had cooked, suddenly didn't agree with her stomach. She immediately felt the need to run to the bathroom to throw up.

Jonathan quickly ran to her side after hearing the unpleasant noises coming from her in the bathroom. Forgetting about breakfast, Jonathan whisked Misty up in his arms and took her to the local hospital. As they waited for the doctor to come with the results of his findings, Jonathan nervously paced back and forth in the waiting area.

Meanwhile, Misty had taken a short nap from all the excitement of the morning. Shortly, the doctor lightly tapped on the room door before entering. After hearing the findings, Misty was once more filled with joy as tears began to stream down her face.

Jonathan was given the green light to go to his wife, only to find her with tears in her eyes, which sent an alarm down his spine. "Misty, what's wrong sweetheart? What did the doctor say? Honey, you're frightening me, what's wrong? Can you please answer me?" Jonathan insisted with a nervousness that Misty hadn't seen before. She immediately understood what was going on with Jonathan and shared the life-changing news with her husband. His eyes lit up with tears of joy at the prospect of having his first child on the way.

Without hesitation, he embraced Misty in his arms, they both shared tears of joy in the hospital before Misty was given instructions and discharged. After arriving home and getting Misty settled, he decided to wait until morning to surprise his parents. But Misty had another idea instead of calling his parents. She shared her idea with Jonathan, and he immediately went to work organizing a grandparent pregnancy reveal party for his parents and Dr. Laura.

It was decided that they all would meet at the local banquet hall for a small family gathering. When he dialed his parents to invite them to the banquet, they were a bit confused at the sudden gathering. His parents quickly arrived at the hall wondering what was going on.

Once inside, they were met with everyone saying, "SURPRISE", with excitement Jonathan and Misty in the front of the hall grinning from ear to ear like Cheshire cats as his parents moved closer to where they were.

Jonathan and Misty could barely contain themselves long enough for his parents to be seated. Finally, the moment came when they had a curtain to drop down from the ceiling of the hall along with balloons and confetti over their parents in the great reveal that they would soon be grandparents for the first time.

His mother's exuberant cry of "Hallelujah!" filled the room, followed by his father's emotional embrace, and tears glistening in his eyes. Dr. Laura also stood by with tears in her eyes for Misty. After catching their breath, celebrating, they joined Misty and Jonathan in hugs and kisses, and then clinked glasses filled with sparkling apple cider, toasting to the new addition to their family.

As thoughts turned to preparations, Misty envisioned a nursery inspired by her childhood surrounded by elephants, monkeys, cheetahs, lions, coyotes, and birds. She desired to have a tall tree painted on one wall and a crib suspended from the ceiling above it.

In planning for the baby's arrival, Misty imagined a cozy space complete with a closet stocked with tiny clothes, throw pillows scattered around for comfort, walkie-talkies for late-night chats between rooms, a dresser for organization, and soft blankets for warmth in either a bassinet or crib. After adjusting to their new role as parents, Jonathan and Misty soon were able to return to work as his parents were the caregivers for their little one when they were away. Because having strangers take care of their child was out of the question, and so they agreed upon only his parents to be the caregivers.

Things were going in such an amazing way for Misty and Jonathan that ten months later, Misty found herself keeled over in the bathroom once more. This time she knew the signs of what was going on, another bundle of joy was on the way.

The End

Author's Final Words

Emerging from a small village that was called home, Misty was suddenly swept away from what was familiar to her in a vast world of unfamiliarity. She clutched onto the few belongings that she had managed to bring with her on her journey to America - a small bundle of clothes and a meager amount of money. There would be no family waiting for her there, and no familiar faces to offer comfort. But Misty knew that she had no other choice but to survive in honor of her lost parents.

Can you imagine stepping into Misty's shoes for just a moment, feeling the weight of uncertainty, fear, and trepidation to reach inside of herself and find strength to go on? For Misty, it took four years of hard work of letting go, and opening up to strangers to be pulled out of a dark place of trauma to that of an overcomer, achiever, and then role model. It is this drive that pushes us to strive for more and do better in life. But for Misty, she can finally exhale and bask in the satisfaction of accomplishing her goals. The path she was given and then chose was not easy, but every step brought her closer to where she needed to be. And now, with each new chapter of her life, she knows that she has the strength and determination to face any challenge that comes her way.

Summary

The story of Misty unfolded with a heart-wrenching awakening to a world engulfed in turmoil. She fled through the chaos, forced to bid farewell to her familiar existence and plunge into an unknown future in America through a prestigious scholarship. Adrift in a foreign land without any connections, she felt like a small boat tossed in a stormy sea. But amidst the uncertainty, she found comfort in a supportive community that embraced her and guided her through life's tumultuous passageways.

Gratitude filled her for the commitment and faith instilled by her upbringing, shaped by the firm yet loving hand of her parents. Misty learned that life requires courage, resilience, tears, and perseverance as she faced its challenges and uncertainties. It's an unpredictable journey with an uncertain destination at the end.

The career she passionately pursued gave her a sense of purpose and fulfillment by allowing her to use her skills to make a positive impact on the lives of others. Each day, as she worked tirelessly to assist those in need, she felt a deep sense of satisfaction and pride in her chosen path.

Misty's life had turned out to be everything she had ever hoped for. She was happily married with two beautiful children, and her husband stood by her side, a pillar of strength and support. They had built a home filled with love and laughter, where memories were made and dreams come true. Misty couldn't have asked for a better life, and every day she counted her blessings as she watched her family flourish and grow. The future held endless possibilities, and she was grateful to experience it all with the ones she loved most.

I am absolutely delighted that you've chosen to stop by and delve into Misty. This captivating tale resonates with women across the globe, touching hearts and inspiring minds.

Follow us on Facebook: Eat-n-Enjoy page

Follow us on Instagram: Eatnenjoy21 page

https://www.etsy.com/shop/KidsAndKidBooks

We have in stock ABCs Board 26 letters, and Number Board 1-30 for children's education purposes.

Title: **(Spanish) La Gran Pesca del Dia \ The Big Catch of the Day**

Title: **The Adventures of Sheila, The Spotted Pig**

Title: **New York City Children Short Stories and Workbook Ages 8-12**

Title: **Dad & Me Coloring & Activity Book Ages 4-6**

Title: **Workbook for Kids of all Ages (Sight Words, Colors and Shapes)**

Title: **Mermaid World Coloring & Activity Book Ages 4-8**

Title: **Mom & Me Coloring & Activity Book for Kids Ages 4-8**

Title: **Unicorn Land Coloring & Activity Book Ages 4-8**

Title: **Letter and Number Tracing Handwriting Practice for Kids Ages 3-6**

Title: **Love From My Little Pals Coloring and Activity Book All Ages**

Title: **Love From My Little Pals Book All Ages**

Title: **Word Search for Kids (Puzzles & Games) Ages 6 & up**

Title: **Stuff Happens!**

Life is full of surprises, especially when it comes to matters of the heart.

Title: **The Street Girl #1**

From the streets to unexpected love, these tales will take you on a wild ride.

Title: **The Keys to my Heart:**

When your spouse means everything to you, and he isn't here anymore. What is a girl to do now without her protector? As each day goes by, my heart bleeds for him.

Title: **Broken Promises**:

"Love shattered, a family torn apart. Can the wounds of the past heal, or will the cycle of pain continue?" The struggle is real, and the desire for success consumes me. I can almost taste it on my tongue—the sweet victory of overcoming challenging times and devastating moments.

Despite countless hours in therapy and sleepless nights studying, I refused to give up my dream, sacrificing the comfort of my own bed. And now, as I walk down the aisle to receive my hard-earned degree, the feeling is indescribable.

It is like climbing a mountain, where every step is a challenge to overcome. But finally reaching the summit and seeing the world from a new perspective makes every struggle and sacrifice worth it. This moment is one of triumph and pride, a chapter closed and a new one beginning.